THE JOURNEY

SUNRISE

THE JOURNEY

SUNRISE

No one is asked to be born into this world. A
child is born because two adults decide to be
either responsible or, irresponsible. Either way,
it has a great effect on the individual.

Barbara-Lee Moulton

To order additional copies of this book, contact:
Xlibris
1-888-795-4274
www.Xlibris.com
Orders@Xlibris.com
782868

To my wonderfully made children,

Naturelle and Wayne Goodluck,

May your days be blessed.

May your purpose in life be fulfilled,

May the Universe work for you positively.

I love you very much.

Mommy

THE JOURNEY
SUNRISE

THE JOURNEY

SUNRISE

Life starts at one point and ends at another. What we experience in it is our story to tell. Some start happy, some start sad, some start mysteriously, some start with a question mark and some start by just starting.

At least those are her thoughts at this moment as she sits this late on the dining table made of polished marble. The lights are so bright over the dining table, because she needs glasses to see the keys on the key board of the computer. The television airing a sports channel that is so loud in her master bedroom, prevents her from hearing the noises outside. She is feeling tire from the usual chaos of the day, so She gets up from the dining table and walks to the front door through the dark living room. On the video deck in the living room shows 10:40 pm. Through the glass panel on the front door, she stood staring into the dark streets riddle with faint lights shining from the light poles. She was in one of the states of America, called Rhode Island. In the city of Johnston, she stood there looking outside, her mind pondering over the mysteries of life.

She walked back to the dining table and sat down to continue her writing, but sleep has no mercy. She heard that from a folklore told her as she was growing up by her grandmother. Sleep is creeping into her eyes now, but she must finish what she is writing. She has been thinking about writing a book for about 32 years now and she is finally giving it a shot. For once, something made her feel a sense of pure joy in her inner spirit. After penning more words, with a smile she gets up and stretch a little, but instead of continuing, she walks toward the bedroom and landed in bed for a sweet and long rest as she didn't have to go to work the next day.

Chapter 1

Comfort Meneh, was sweeping the yard for the last time during that day before retiring for the evening. That was the routine for the Meneh family. Everyday, the eldest child or anyone chosen will clean the yard and make sure that everything was packed in its proper place before retiring to bed. She picked up the bench and took it to the corner of the house. As she bends to put the bench down she felt a sharp pain in her lower back. She tried to stand upright but the pain could not allow that. Martha Wleh, Comfort's mother, who was still seated at the entrance of the front door waiting for her daughter to finish cleaning, noticed her daughter and She asked in her native dialect if everything was okay. Comfort shook her head sideways indicating that all was not well.

Martha got up and walked over to where Comfort was and rub her back soothingly. It took some minutes for Comfort to feel better, and all was okay again.

Martha helped her finish the cleaning. They went inside and Martha being a woman of experience told her to pack some things, they had to get to the hospital.

Comfort had a friend whose dad drove a taxi cab for a living. She called her and asked for her father's service. The cab arrived at 8:30 pm and Martha and Comfort got in to make the trip to the hospital. The hospital was about 15 minutes away from where they live. When They arrived at the hospital, they thanked and paid the driver and got out of the cab. Comfort stood for a while, looking at the entrance of the hospital, she stood frozen. It has just hit her the reason for her being there, she did not know what it was like to give birth.

Her mother took her arm and pull her toward the entrance of the hospital. Inside, they walked to the registration window. The registry for the night shift looked up and ask how she could be of help. Comfort give the registry her name and told her that she was due in anytime that week. After taking her information, the lady usher Comfort and her Mother in the waiting room.

The waiting room was fill with older women and young girls, all waiting to see their doctors for different reasons. It was so noisy in here, everyone talking or whispering something to the other. The waiting room consisted of a pharmacy, lots of benches, and a counter where numbers were assigned to patients and patients chart was found and taken to the Doctor. She and her mother waited anxiously for the call. 5 minutes went by, 10 minutes, 15 minutes, finally a nurse came in and called in a loud voice "Comfort Nemeh". She and her Mother got up and follow the direction of the nurse. They entered a room. It was a singer room, a bed against the wall, a table, a chair for a guest and a bathroom. Although there was a door, the hospital kept it open always in case of emergency. The nurse told her to sit on the bed for her pressure to be taken. With a smile, she said to Comfort "although you know who I am, but in this hospital, I have to formally introduce myself." She then stretched out her hand to Comfort "My name is Angela Fey, and I am the head nurse here." The Doctor will be in shortly to see you, but first I must take your blood pressure, she said as she proceeded to take Comfort blood pressure. The reading of her blood pressure was good the nurse told her and encourage her to lay down and rest. "I will be checking on you from time to time." Comfort smiled and thanked the nurse. "If there is an emergency please press this button on the side of the bed head and we will come over quickly." said the nurse again. Comfort nodded her head in agreement and the nurse then left the room.

She sat on the bed wondering where Sephan Soul was. She had not heard from him for months now. Although she was hurt, emotionally and they were not on the best of terms, she still hopes that he would show some concern. She had not bargain for this nor was she prepare for it. She sat there thinking, how something that felt so right could go wrong. It was a little over 7 minutes when the Doctor came in to see her. He checked her blood pressure again and did other examinations. Everything looked good. "You should be ready anytime from now", he told her and reassured her that the nurses would be available for her with the button at her finger tip. She smiled and nodded again. "Thank you Doctor," she said with a shaky voice.

She sat there on the bed edge and talked with her mother. She asked her mother about what it was like for the mother the first time. Her mother told her some stories to keep her from being frighten. This was the first time for Comfort, she was young, frighten and had no experience in these matters. Her mother told her to lay down and rest because she would need the strength to push the baby out. She obeyed and was fast asleep before her mother could end the other story.

At about 4:00am a pain stronger than the first woke her up. She stiffens and made these funny sounds. She reached the button but decided against it as the pain seams to disappeared. She lies back down. What she didn't know was that the nurses were checking on her all the time while she was asleep. 5:00am another pain hit her. Stronger than the one before. Just as she was about to fall asleep another pain hit. This time the pain was so heavy, she did not hesitate, she pressed the button. she was making all kind of sounds this time around. Her mother who was sleeping in the chair not far from the bed, jumped to her side. She told her mother she wanted to use the toilet, but her mother told her to wait for the nurse. The nurse came in and rush to her bedside to prevent her from standing up. She told the nurse that she really needed to use the toilet. The nurse told her that she had to check her first before allowing her to go to the rest room. Pressing her back down in bed the nurse checked her and said it is time. You do not need the toilet. The nurse rolls her out of the room into another room. This room was empty of people. Just instruments. The pain was on and off at an interval of 30 seconds. The pain was not reducing but getting frequent. The Doctor came in by 6:10am with another nurse. Greetings were exchange and the Doctor started to give his instructions. Within 10 minutes a sound of a baby cry rang through the room. A beautiful baby girl, the Doctor announced. Comfort smiled as she heard the cry of her baby. She was about to thank the Doctor when a sharp pain hit her again. She was getting short of breath. The Doctor asked her "what are you feeling?" He did not wait for her answer as he went ahead to check and complete his work. He was shocked. 'There is another baby on its way", he announced. Comfort was just as shocked, but Martha Wleh was happy and dancing. There was a single heartbeat when he checked, and her chart said nothing about twins. Those were his thoughts as he guided the other baby out. "Another girl" he said. A third nurse was called in. This time he checked her again because he did not want any more surprises. He finished his work and instructed the nurse to finish cleaning her up and returned her to her room.

A nurse took her to her room while the other nurses took the babies to the nursery. It wasn't long before Comfort was fast asleep in her room from exhaustion. Martha followed the nurses to the nursery window to look at the babies. She was peeking through the nursery window as the nurses finished cleaning and lay the little ones down. She could not wait to hold her grand children in her arms.

Somewhere in the hospital, a telephone call was made to an outside location. The nurse said in the telephone, "she has given birth to two girls." The lady on the other end of the line was so silent that You could have heard a pin drop if it fell to the floor. It was like the person on the other end of the line stopped breathing. The nurse then repeatedly said "hello, hello" but she heard the click from the other end as the line went dead. The nurse stood starring at the phone and wondering what has just happen? She tried calling again but this time the telephone just rang.

Chapter 2

The morning was cold and breezy, but you could see from the distance the sun was under the clouds about to shine in all its glory. He walked to his Toyota Land Cruiser. He loves this SUV because he was a rough rider. He took good care of his baby as he refers to the white SUV and his baby took good care of him. Though the roads were all dirt roads, he made sure the SUV was clean after every day's work.

Today was not like other days. today Sephan Soul was traveling to a new region to make assessment for relocation as his work sometimes imposes on him. Dressed in his dark jean trouser and light blue jeans shirt and a pair of brown shoes. Although, he worked on the field, he was always dressed like a model ready for the run way. Sephan Soul was light skin, 5 feet and 11 inches tall, he was a handsome young man. Every where he went the ladies asked about him. He was what the old people called a head turner.

Sephan Soul graduated from an American College where he made his mark as an honored student. Top of his class. He went back home to put in practice and contribute to his country what he had learned as an engineer. He loved his career and he worked with passion and enthusiasm. He was so full of energy and youth was on his side.

He was the first of several children of a middle-class family. His parents taught him all the good values in life about how to be respectful but ambitious. They taught him to be responsible at an early age because he was the head of the family in the African tradition. He would one day take the parents position to care for his younger one when the parents were dead. He took those responsibility seriously.

He walked to the driver side and open the door. He put one foot in the SUV and looked up in the sky. Smiling at how beautiful the sky looked he said a little prayer as he always did anytime he got in the SUV. He turned the ignition and pop the hood of the jeep. He went around to the front as a boy who usually goes with him on these trips, opened the hood. Together, they checked the oil, water, sound of the engine and fan belt and what other thing needed checking. Everything looked good so far. They closed the hood and the boy proceeded to putting the luggage's in the back of the SUV.

Sephan Soul turned the ignition off and then started it again. The boy got in the passenger side of the SUV, put his seat belt on. Mr. Soul turned to the boy and said, "Are you ready?" James shook his head up and down indicating yes. Mr. soul closed his door put his seat belt on and pressed the accelerator. They were on their way to the southeastern part of the country.

James Edwards was a young boy who got attached to Mr. Soul on one of the building construction projects. This young man admired the boss so much and was always running to the SUV whenever it pulled up on the site. He would take the boss brief case and carry it to where ever the boss wanted it. He would make sure that whatever the boss wanted was quickly available if he could provide it. Mr. Soul liked his attitude and decided to take him as a son on the job.

The day was getting warm as the sun started to show up gradually. Sephan was once more about to work his magic on the road. He pressed on the accelerator as if he already mastered the road to his destination. They had a long way to go as they were headed to another county called Maryland.

Maryland is a beautiful county found in the south eastern part of the country Liberia located in West Africa. Its Capital city is Harper. This county was named after the state of Maryland in the united states of America.

Walking toward her home somewhere in Harper city, Maryland county, was this dazzling beauty in her teens. She was heavy bones, 5 feet 7 inches tall. Where ever she went, whether it was at school, at a party, to the market, or in the towns to do a little selling, she was a sight for the sore eyes. The people she encountered loved her. Her friends envied her, but still admired her. People that saw her for the first time thought she was from a rich family because she looked so radiant. Even those that knew her sometimes forgot that she came from a poor background. She was multi-tasking by selling goods and going to school. She sold African lapel to her friends and the town folks after school, then went home to help her mother with the house work. She studied every day after she was finished with her house work. She was loving, caring, ambitious, outgoing and yet naïve. She was named Comfort Nemeh by her mother's sister who lived in Ivory Coast which was their neighbor.

Comfort was the first child of her parents. Coming from an African descent, being the first child and being a girl for your parents didn't count for much. Boys were preferred because they are the head of household and they were the ones to grow the family name. The father felt like the mother had failed him by not giving him a son as the head of the family. This made Comfort's position difficult as she had to struggle for her father's affection.

She was about 7 years when her father walked out on the family, leaving the mom to take care of four children. They did little farming to sustain the family, but this was not enough to send the children to school. Comfort Nemeh had already started school and she liked it and cried to her mother to keep her in school. Her mother who was uneducated but knew that education was important assured her daughter that she would go to school. They needed to plant more food stuff and be able to sell them to get a little more money to afford the tuition for her school. This made her mother stay in the field longer than usual. She had to work harder to be able to meet up with her promise.

As Comfort got older she saw and felt the pains of her mother and decided that she had to do something to help her mother. Here she was, selling her own goods to stay in school after all these years. The land did well over the years in production, but it was not big enough to take care of all of them. There was not much the land could offer as support for the family and her school anymore because as she grew older, somethings changed, her life style changed, tuition got higher and even the economic situation in the country changed.

She was the pillar of the family, the one who was getting an education. She was kind and caring for her family, not only her mother and siblings but also for her extended family. They looked up to her and was proud of her. She was their hero and she liked that.

Vacation was the favorite time of year, when they could rest from getting up too early to walk to school, or study for test, or stay up late to do home work with candle lights or lanterns. She and her friends will crush every party in the town. They call it advertising because they met people and told them about their business. They also showed off the latest fashion as part of their business plan. Comfort and her group of friends were the talk of the town. They never wore the same cloth twice. They were known as the classic book girls.

At about late afternoon, the next day, Mr. Soul and James arrived after a long and rough ride. His host who was called Catrina, a prominent lady in that part of the country and another friend greeted them as they stepped out of the vehicle. They exchange pleasantries and the host invited them in. She showed Mr. Soul to his room and took James to the boy's quarter and showed him his room. "When you are settle in, come to the kitchen, the maid will give you some food." She told him. She went back into the house and yelled to Sephan, "food is ready." Catrina Otto went back to the living room where Mr. Nathaniel Jimeson who was a close friend of Sephan and a common friend to he and Catrina was waiting. They chatted for a while catching up on old times as she had not seen him for awhile also. Jokingly, she stated, "I know that I will be seeing you now that your friend is here". They laughed about it.

When Sephan returned to the living room he was relaxed. He had showered and put on a T-shirt and jeans. He wore a more casual feet ware because with his friend around, there was no time to waste on sleep. After a late lunch, they would take a spin around the town. Mr. soul was more of an action man. He was young and full of energy and he wanted to experience and enjoy life. The saying goes "All work and no play makes Jack a dull boy" He was not going to be Jack.

They move to the dining room table where he found his favorite dish. Dry rice and fried fish. This is an African dish. Contrary to its name, this dish includes smoked pork, smoked fish, luncheon meat or spam, a bit of okra, bitter ball, some pepper sauce, palm oil and fried fish. There are various versions of this dish. There were other foods on the table but that was what he wanted to eat.

As they ate, they talked about themselves. About their work and other stuff. Sephan asked if James was given food. "yes" Catrina replied. When they finished eating, they sat around drinking tea and talking.

Sephan and Nathaniel decided to go around town site seeing in the early evening. They drove through the main streets in the city. Nathaniel promise to pick him up in the morning to give him a real toll. Later they stopped at a local bar to meet up with some other friends. They sat down and order drinks. They talked about the time when they were in school and joke each other. The waiter brought their drinks. The music was mild and there were other people in different areas of the bar. They all seem to be having a good time.

"The day has been a long and enjoyable one gentleman, but I must retire to rest for tomorrow is another day," Sephan said. His friends laugh but agreed. He and Nathaniel said goodnight to their friends and left. When they drove up in front of the house of the host, Sephan got out of the vehicle, said "thanks and see you tomorrow." When Catrina opened the door for Sephan, he thanked her and told her that he was tired. He headed straight for his room and jumped into bed. Before long, he was fast asleep.

The sun streaks passing through the window blinds and shining directly on his face as he turned on the bed, woke him up. Sephan stretched his body across the bed and sat up. He had slept all through the night, he now realized how tired he had been. He quickly showered, got dressed and went to the living room. Nathaniel and Catrina were already at the dining table having coffee. Sephan said his morning greetings and took his seat. He fills his cup with tea and took a sip. Catrina asked if he had a good night rest? He did he said. They chatted and ate breakfast. When they finish, Catrina said she was going about her business for the day. Sephan and Nathaniel got up and went outside. James was already by the vehicle waiting for them. They all got in the vehicle and Nathaniel was on his way to the city.

Harper is a beautiful city. A city of the County Maryland in Liberia, west Africa. The free African slaves of America settled on this beautiful Coast line area in the 1800s.

Sephan relocation survey was in line with the contract to construct and build suitable high ways to link Counties. A job he loves doing. Sephan and Nathaniel drove through the towns and he observed the road system. They had lunch at a local Restaurant and at the end of the day's tour went home for dinner. In the evening they went out as usual but visited different bars for small talk with friends.

Chapter 3

She was a beauty to behold. Black and 5 feet 7 inches tall, a pleasant and shy smile, a presence that was too strong to go unnoticed. Comfort wore her uniform and took her copybooks. The school year was coming to an end and she must make sure to stay an honor rolled student. She was always on time but this morning she was running a little late. She spent most of the night studying for her exams. She dashes out of the house forgetting to go to her mother's room.

Everyone was seated in class waiting for the test papers to be shared when she arrived. She took her seat as the teacher was distributing the test papers. She started working as soon as hers was handed to her. She wrote her name and read over the questions. She worked the easy one first and went on to the difficult ones. Not so difficult she thought. Apart from recess the rest of the day was exams.

After school Comfort and some friends walked in group and discuss the answers of the exams. They argued the wrong and right answers. Some of them were worried and some knew what they had done. Comfort knew that she had study and even if she did not make 100% she was going to get a high score. Some of her friends wanted to go walk about for a while but she said she would rather go home and study. She did not want to worry about her grades.

Her mother, Martha Wleh was finish cooking and was doing a little clean up job when she got home. "Hello" she spoke to her mother and went inside to put her copybooks down. She changes into her casual clothes and went straight for food. After eating she help her mother get the rest of the place and dishes clean. She helps put water on the fire, so the other children could take bath before bedtime. The older ones would bath themselves while she would help to bath the younger ones. She went outside, under the tree to study for her exam.

Her business would have to wait until after her exams. She needed more lapels to add to her collection for sale and that meant that she had to go to the neighboring country to get goods. Cote D'Ivoire, a French speaking country was across the river. She made It a week's journey to go and come back home. She enjoyed doing the business. it was interesting and rewarding for her.

She got her little siblings ready for bed as darkness lasted longer because there was not electricity for them. She took her bath also and continue with her study inside with the light of a lantern. When her eyes could no longer stand the pressure of sleep, she gave up and went to bed.

It was Friday, the last day of the exam. She could not wait for the exam to end today. She was starting to get a headache from too much reading. She got ready and went to school. She got in early and had time to read over her notes.

Her girlfriend, Nancy Logan asked her what they were going to do after the exam, and Comfort said that they would walk about, maybe visit her favorite Aunt. They took their exams and by the time it was over, her headache had increase. At the end of school, she told Nancy that she needed to sleep her headache off, therefore, she was not able to go around with her. She went home, and her mother boiled some herbs for her to inhale. Hoping that it will help her headache disappear.

On Saturday, Nancy came to visit her, but she was still under the weather.

Sunday came, and she was much better. When Nancy came around, they were able to discuss about their travel to the neighboring country for their business. Nancy told her that her goods were still not finish yet, so she did not think she would make the trip. This came as a disappointment for Comfort as she always travels with her friend. They later went to another friend's house for chit chat. The time went by so fast when having fun with her friends. It was time for Comfort to head back home.

The final exams were here, and this was always an intense period. After the final exams, there is usually no major activities in the study department at school. Some children went to school lazily, while others continue their enthusiasm. Comfort asked to be excuse from school at this time to get her goods. Once granted she was on her way the next day. She got to Cote D'Ivoire and went to her play mother's house. She was always welcome warmly by this lady who befriended her on her first visit to this country. Since then, this has been her stopping point. Patience would take her to the market the next day and give her all the information about the new things in style. Patience was a business woman too and had an eye for fashion. With her help Comfort took back the new things that were in style. This give comfort an edge in the business back home as she loves good things. Shopping was always fun. She met new business people and increased her experience. Everyday she will go to the market to shop and when she was done, she would go to Patience business spot to wait until closing time. While there she would pick up tips from Patience by just watching her interact with her customers.

Three days went by so fast that she hardly noticed. It was time to get back. She did not want to miss any activities in school. The next day she was all set to get back to Pleebo, her home town.

This morning was a very tensed day. It was the day of the national exams. If you did not pass these exams you would have to take it again the following year. That was considered a failure to you and your loved ones. Some students formed groups to go over what they had study. Some were looking for food, some drinks. It was a rush. The bell rang out so loud that some student's hearts begin to pound. They took their seats to focus on the exams. Exams papers were shared, and student begin to work. Five hours had passed, bringing the exams to an end. The students were all relief hoping they had all done their best. Comfort was quite relief. She already knew she was in the passing group. She could not wait to be in Senior high school. She had come a long way and so she looked up and thanked God to herself. She gathers her group and took toward the town as it was customary, they wrote all over their uniforms, allowing their friend to sign on the shirts. They would walk all over town and make noise while visiting family members and friends. People would congratulate them for their hard work done in accomplishing the next level in school. It was a fun time for them. Comfort was super happy for her Mother will be Proud.

Chapter 4

A week tour around the County was quite rewarding. Sephan gather his findings about his project and was ready to head back to his previous location. His host has been wonderful and his friends also. The boys gather one last time before his departure the next day. He left them early because a lot was on his mind. He was so excited about this assignment.

He woke up to the aroma of his favorite dish. He got out of bed, bathed and dressed. When he got outside the table was set with European breakfast. "I thought I smell some dried rice and fried fish?" he said. Catrina then told him that indeed there was dried rice and fried fish for him to take on his trip back. He gave her a hug and told her she was the best. They sat and ate. He thanked his host and took off on his journey.

Getting back to Sinoe safely was a relief. It was very dark when they arrived, it was early morning the next day. He thought to himself; today is another day, I am tired, and he went on to sleep. When he woke up, it was still mid-morning, the day was young. He put the light on and sat at the table in the corner of his room to go over his report. The day was going to be a long one. The report was to be presented, discussed and concluded.

The report went well. In two weeks he was relocating. He had to complete this project within one week and get ready to relocate. There was not much left to do on the project anyway. He went to work vigorously to finish up what he had to complete.

Sephan Soul called James. "you know that this weekend we are relocating to Maryland, I want you to be very attentive on the site as all the equipment will be taken with us. We must make sure that everything is packed. I do not want to rush on the last minute, therefore we will start packing and loading the equipment today." James assured him that he would be attentive and was ready to work along with the other workers.

It was the day before his departure, a send off party was held for him by his friends. The people in the county loved him so much and thanked him for his work and kindness. He carried himself like a son of the soil. At the end of it all, he thanked them for their warm reception of him and his work force and hope that he and the workers could have done even more. The evening was enjoyable, but he was a bit nausea from too much food and drinks. He was going to missed them. These were good people.

Sephan woke up the next morning with feeling energetic and ready to hit the road. James was at the SUV waiting for his instructions. They arrived in Maryland later then a normal trip because of the heavy machineries and the condition of the road. They had to work late into the morning to unload some important items in the ware house. The employees were then shown were they would reside until the project was over.

At 3:00 in the morning, Mr. Soul and James got to the house that Mr. soul had chosen on the cape. A beautiful house standing on a green and well-groomed field. He was too tired and sleepy to enjoy any view. Catrina had told him to pass by her house to eat but that would have to wait until late afternoon because it was now too late.

Later that day, He was up by 8:00am and got ready to go to work. On his way he stopped by Catrina house and left his house keys. She was to put some things in place for him. She was usually up by 5:00am every morning. She told him that she was going to take care of his food until he got settled in. He thanked her for her kindness. She had breakfast ready for him, but he decided to take it with him because he had too much to do. If he sat down now to eat breakfast with her, she would open a conversation and that would take a while. He thanked her also for the breakfast and went to his office.

At the office he sat down and drank the tea. He called James and give him the rest of the breakfast. He started working on organizing his office and putting paper and documents where they belong. Tomorrow he will have to brief his colleagues at the office about his work plans and give them the listing of things he needed immediately to start the project. He called in some of the workers and give them the assignment for the day. James came back in his office after he finished eating to help him settle the office. By the time the clock struck 12:00, the office was in good shape and Sephan was behind his desk jotting things down. He told James to go and start the car so that they go and have lunch with Catrina.

They got to Catrina house and she came to open the door. She told James to pass around the house to enter the kitchen where she had food store for him. She jokingly told Sephan that he would pay for her food from the previous night. He laughed and told her that he would. They got to the table and sat down to eat some fry potatoes greens and rice. He told her that as soon as they were finish eating, he would call Nathaniel. She said that Nathaniel had not been there but had called her twice to check on her. "it would be the weekend before I even try to see him, I am too busy setting up". Catrina told him all she had done at the house and said that she will continue after lunch. He thanked her again.

After lunch, on his way back to his office he called Nathaniel. They chatted all the way to his office. Nathaniel told him that he was dropping everything and coming to the site, but he pleaded with him that they should meet over the weekend. He got to the office and went on an inspection pertaining to what the workers had done. He checked the ware house and around the entire place, briefing people here and there as to what was expected of them. Sephan went back to his office and compiled the day's report. He was tire and needed to get a long night sleep. He called Catrina for his house keys and she said, she was home. He passed by her house and collected his house keys. She told him that she had taken food at his house. He thanked her and left her house.

When Sephan open his house door and went inside, he was impress with what Catrina had done with the interior decoration. He walked all through the house and he liked it. She had taste he thought. He called her and thanked her and told her how much he liked what she had done there. He told James to put his bags down and check in the kitchen for food before going to the boy's quarter.

Every morning Sephan and James will have breakfast at home or at Catrina's house before going to work. They always needed the energy as they burned a lot of energy moving around from inspecting areas to checking equipment's. They were always busy doing something. It was never a dull moment. At the end of the day they were all so exhausted.

It was nearing the end of the year and Sephan was progressing with the project. He went out with his friends every weekend to refresh himself for the next working week. He has been doing that for the past months. On this weekend, he got home by 1:00am. He had a bad headache, he had too much to drink. He got home and rush to his master bathroom. He changed to his robe, came out and threw himself on the bed. He then noticed that someone was in his bed. He looked at her and realized it was Catrina. He was so exhausted and drunk that he was not alarmed by it. He lied down and pull the covers over him. Catrina was pretending to be asleep. Sephan wondered what she was doing in his bed. He thought about waking her up, but she looked so peaceful while sleeping, he decided not to wake her up. He just wanted to sleep. She should have a good explanation in the morning. He drifted from his thoughts into sleep.

Oh shit! he is having a nightmare, or, so he thought; he felt the tender hands of a lady stroking his chest and moving slowly over his body. He started to warm up to the feeling and he liked how it felt. He was being kissed behind the ears and his body was responding. He turned and started to kiss back. His heart was raising, and he felt his chest expanding back and forth. It felt so good, he did not want it to stop. This ignited the passion with in him and he took control of the situation and started making love to her. tenderly caressing her at first and then taking her with a burning desire. They were panting as if they had run a marathon after reaching a climax. He got up and went in the bathroom, when he got through urinating, that is when it hit him that he had just made love to Catrina. It was not a nightmare after all. Now he was embarrassed to go back inside the room. How can he face her? She was older than he and she seduced him. He was confused. He stayed in the bathroom going through his morning routine and even staying longer than usual. Catrina called out to him and told him that she was leaving. He answered "okay." when he got out of the bathroom, Catrina was gone. He sat on his bed, put his face in the palm of his hands and bowed. What has just happened? He wondered.

Catrina fixed breakfast for him before she left. She felt good this morning. She had made her conquest and she intended to do anything to keep him, although she was older than him. She was a prominent woman in the society and most people called her mommy as a form of respect.

He called Nathaniel and told him to come over for breakfast. When Nathaniel arrived, Sephan was on the porch drinking some tea. They went into the house and sat at the dining table. Over breakfast, He told Nathaniel what had happened between he and Catrina. Nathaniel told him that he was not surprised. He could tell that the woman had interest from the first time Sephan stayed at her house. Nathaniel teased him, "you are in trouble my friend, you now have a sugar mommy" he laughed. "this is serious, and you are laughing, that was not supposed to happen" Sephan commented. They talked for a while and decided to enjoy the day hanging out with other friends by joining them in a bar.

Chapter 5

It was the first day of school, Senior High School and Comfort could not wait to get on the school grounds. She was too excited this morning. She bathed and got dressed. Her uniform and shoes sparkling of newness. She picked up her book bag and went to her mother's room. "morning mama, I am going to school" (in her dialect). Martha Wleh smile and lifted her hands up as a sign of praise to God. "God bless and protect you my child" she said in her native tongue. Comfort hugged her mother and ran out of the house.

The first day of school was crazy. Students all in a hurry to find their classes and get the best seats. Comfort found a seat in the third row, two seats from the left of the class. She put her book bag down and sat as she, like the others, waited in anticipation to meet their teachers.

School ended for the day and Comfort and her girlfriend walked home. "the math and science teachers were good. I liked most of the teachers though," bertha nyensua told Comfort. "I liked most of the teachers too except for the literature teacher that looks like he has sleeping sickness," they laughed. "he will ask you to read and while you are reading, his head is falling to sleep" comfort continue. "how can his head fall asleep? Just say he fell asleep," Bertha told her. Comfort laughed so hard and said "what can you say about a man who fall asleep when he is standing up? I am telling you only his head fell asleep." they laughed. "you are crazy "Bertha said, as she gives comfort a body shove.

They ran to Comfort house and ate the food Martha had cooked. Comfort changed her uniform. She wore a nice African dress that she bought in ivory coast. She gathers her traveling bag that she usually sells in and turn to leave. They were going to Bertha house so that she would change also.

Bertha asked, "who has the sewing machine in your room?" "me." replied Comfort. "when did you learn how to sew?" "I did not know that you could sew." Bertha continued. "I can't but I will learn, that is why I bought the machine," Comfort told Bertha. She grabbed her bag and they were on their way.

The year 1968 was beginning to show good signs. Their sales went well. Tomorrow is another day, so they had to bring the sales to an end. Comfort said, "I wish sales could be like this every day of the year". "If business work that way, everybody will have money," Said Bertha. "so true my sister, but unfortunately it does not. See you in school tomorrow" Comfort told her.

The morning was cold. He did not want to go anywhere. For once too much partying made him fatigued. It was the day after his birthday. Catrina threw a party for him, though it was not what he wanted but had to go along with it anyway. Nathaniel came with his new girlfriend to the party. "hey Bob, as Sephan was referred to by his close friends, happy birthday. Meet Angela my love." Sephan took her hand and said, "nice to meet you". Angela smiled and said, "happy birthday." Nathaniel took her to meet Catrina and they clicked right away. A lot of people attended and made the party loud. He wished he could escape this party but too many of his good friends were around. They ate and drank and talked and laughed. At about three in the morning, he couldn't take it anymore, so he decided to slip out. Only Nathaniel and his best friend, Tode Davison, who had come from the Monrovia head office, saw him go. People were too busy enjoying themselves to be on the lookout for him. The party went on until the morning with breakfast attached to it.

Work was something he did not play around with. The field got hotter by the hour as the sun was rising to its peak. It was harder to work in very hot weather, but the Roads had to be done. The projects were all coming along well. Sephan was between Monrovia, the capital of Liberia and Maryland County. Sometimes a meeting would require his presence and the communication reached him late evening. He would have to do a mid-morning trip to Monrovia. It sounds stressful but that was why he was the best because he took those situations as a challenge. He loves his job. It was exciting, unexpected and he had to make it work.

He closed early from work and picked Tode up from the house. "you are strong my man" said Tode. I could not wake up this morning." "my man, I heard you come in at 6:30 this morning, so when did you expect to get up" Sephan asked? "but you and I have gone out before and we came in at 5:am and by 7:am you went to work" Tode said. "well, sometimes sleep is hard to come when a million things are running through your mind". "so, what's with you and that lady? She seems nice" Tode said. "yes, she is nice. She likes me, and I respect her but that is it". Tode said, "you have to be careful because those kinds can be over protective". "she knows I respect her, so I go along not to hurt her feelings but for love, no." Sephan said.

Sephan and Tode got down from the SUV and went in to see Catrina. She came running to hug him as if she was a teenager who had not seen her boyfriend for a while. Greetings were exchanged and Sephan thanked her for the party. She said not to bother about it because he was also so generous. Despite the age difference and the fact that he was not in love for marriage, he was a kind-hearted person. He did not mind sharing with his friend and people who showed him love and even people that he did not know. His friends would do anything for him because he made sure that everything was working for them. Catrina said she had something to discuss with him and that would require some time. Sephan looked at Tode with a shy smile. He knew that Catrina would not let him disappear from her today. Tode said "okay I have to see someone, I will take the car and pick you up later". Without anything more to say, Tode rushed out of the house.

It was the middle of the school year and Comfort was relaxed as always when it came to make her grades. Vacation before the second semester was on. This evening, she was on her way to one of her customer. Mary Wolo was one popular woman in the County because of her restaurant and bar.

SOMETHING, as it was call was a spot for middle class people. Comfort went to see her twice a week for payment on goods that Mary took from her and today was no exception. She always put on her best whenever she was going to the Restaurant.

Comfort walked with her head held high, stepping as if she was on the run way.

When she arrived at the restaurant, Mary was behind the counter trying to put some things in order. She looked up with a smile as Comfort came closer. "I know that you won't miss this day for collection Comfort. Said Mary. Just sit and wait for."

He spotted her from the distance as he sat in one corner on the porch of SOMETHING. He gave his friend a notch of the head showing her direction. They both stared until she was at the counter. He picked up his bottle of stout and put it to his lips. He took a big swallow with his eyes still fixed on her. He must get to know her, he must talk to her. Should he go over there, or should he wait and follow her when she's leaving? His mind was juggling all these different thoughts. He heard his friend laugh, that brought his mind back to the real world. "what?" he asks. "relax man, she is doing business with Mary, stop staring like that." Nathaniel said. "so, what does that means?" Ask Sephan again. "that means, you can ask Mary who she is." Said Nathaniel. They both laughed.

Comfort and Mary ended their transaction and Comfort walked out the restaurant. Sephan got up to follow her but his friend stopped him. "Mary please come and sit with your customer, we are missing you" Nathaniel yelled. "I will be with you shortly" she replied. The girl behind the counter return and Mary than walked over to Nathaniel and Sephan table. She took her seat in the middle of them and smile. "is everything all right?" "everything is fine". Said Nathaniel. "Mary, who was the girl, wearing the short jeans pants and pink blouse that you were talking with a while ago?" "ah ha! I knew you did not call me for nothing. Her name is Comfort and she sells clothes to me at times." "how can I meet her?" Sephan said for the first time. "two weeks from today she will be here again. I will introduce her to you". "two weeks from now is too long, I could have introduced myself today if you had not stopped me." Said Sephan to Nathaniel. "now all the blame is going on me. I am sorry." said Nathaniel.

The next two weeks were tough. Sephan could not get the image of her out of his mind. He started checking the days until he would meet her. He had to attend a meeting in Monrovia the end of the week, but he hoped to be back before Comfort meeting with Mary. The road trip was a little tough as it was the raining season. He arrived in Monrovia safely. The next day he went to brief his superior of the successes and hitches that the project was faced with. A budget was set for the next phase of the project. He would have to wait for two weeks to get the money for the project.

On his way back, he bought a clutch for her, hoping to see her. As soon as he got back from Monrovia, he checked at SOMETHING to see if she had stopped by. Mary told him that she had not come back since that day. He felt disappointed as he left. He hoped to run into her on his way but that was just hope. He went to work everyday and had fun with his friends but some how the image of the girl found its way in his mind.

The morning was a bit slow, he felt a slight headache from the night before. He walked to the bath cabinet and took two tablets and threw them in his mouth. He went in the kitchen and got some water from the freezer and swallow the pills. That should do the trick, he thought. The month of October always caught him off guard. He was sometimes energetic and some days he felt like something was draining his energy. The first of October felt like he was in for a tough ride of the month. He tried to get ready as fast as he could, grabbed a quick breakfast and was on his way.

It was drizzling outside at first, then it started to rain cats and dogs. The unpredictability of October had started to show its head already. Instead of driving the short cut to his office, he decided to take the main street. Few yards down the road, he noticed a girl running in the rain to get to a shelter. She must have been caught in the rain unaware. He blew the car horn and ask to give her a lift. When she stopped and looked at him, his heart stopped for a few seconds. He was looking at the girl that took his breath away the first time he saw her. She thought, what harm could he do her in the light of day? It was raining but people were around, people did see him stop, with those thoughts, she got into the jeep. "thank you" she said. He was lost for words. He was too afraid to say the wrong thing. "where are you going?" he asked. "I am reaching to the market". "what is your name" he asked. "Comfort Nemeh." "what is your name?" she said to him. "Sephan Soul" he replied. "nice to meet you Mr. Soul." She said. "please call me Sephan." he told her. "I have seen you before, you do business with Mary that owns SOMETHING," He told her. "yes, she is my customer," Comfort told him. "I should be seeing her this week". "what time this week?" Sephan asked. "on Friday" she replied. "I will be going there also on Friday at about 5:00 in the evening. Could you wait for me please when you get there? I want us to talk." "okay." Comfort said. There was dead silence in the jeep. "please stop me here" she said. He stopped, and she got out. "Thanks" before he could say, welcome, she was gone. He ponders awhile that his day could not have gone any better. Maybe, he needs to change his perception about October after all. His day had just started to look bright.

He went through the week feeling a certain calm. The project had a little set back, but it was nothing that could not be handle. He was feeling too good inside to let the government not sending some equipment's needed for the work to spoil his mood. There is other work to be done. He would move to those yet until the equipment's arrived.

Comfort made some good collections of debts owe to her during the week. She was optimistic about the business. She had started sewing little girl's dresses and the sales were improving little by little. Although she started practicing what her play mother had shown her concerning the sewing process during the first semester, she was starting to be good at it and loving it also. She can see herself getting to where she wanted to be. She hoped to be a graduate and work amongst the elites.

It was Friday afternoon, time to make the Friday round. She had a schedule to collect money from customers that credited from her. On Wednesday and Friday. Today she was going to make SOMETHING (Mary's Bar) the last stop because she was to also meet up with Sephan Soul. She got dressed in a nice black jean pant and a colorful light sweater like blouse with matching sandals. She loves her afro hair style that she always wore out. It makes her look chic.

Every time Comfort dresses, sometimes moderately, like today, she was always a head turner. No matter which way she did it. People would notice this young lady when she enters a room. The looks and compliments would start as soon as she got outside her home. Today was no different. She made her rounds and was successful so far. She got to SOMETHING and went to the counter to ask for Mary. The girl behind the counter pointed at Mary in the far Corner of the bar. "you can go there, she is expecting you." the girl said. "okay, thanks." Comfort got up and walked to were Mary was, then she realized that it was Sephan Soul she was sitting with. "hello" she said. "hello beautiful" Sephan responded. "Sit down." Mary told her. "when you are about to leave, pick it up from the counter." Mary said to her as she left the table. "okay, thanks." said Comfort as she sat down opposite Sephan.

The sun had disappeared. The evening was getting cooler because darkness was fast approaching. "what would you like to drink" Sephan asked. "I will have a soda" she said. He called the waiter to put in their orders. He was drinking stout as usual. Sephan laid back in his chair and introduced himself properly. "I like to know you better, tell me a little about yourself" Sephan Said. "I don't know how to answer that, if I had known that I was coming for an interview, I would have prepared." Comfort reacted. "oh no, don't get me wrong, I just want to know a little about you. For example; are you in school? where do you stay? Something like that." "well, my name is Comfort Nemeh, I am a high school student, I live in Harper city here and I do a little selling." Comfort told him. "you see? that was not hard at all." Sephan said to her. She smiled and looked at him. The waiter brought their drinks and served them.

The night went so fast without them noticing. They clicked after a while and started enjoying each other company. Their conversation flowed so easily, it was like they had known the other for a long time. They started joking and laughing so hard from each other's experiences that she forgot the time. They order some roasted food and ate. She was tired by 11:00 pm. "I have to get home now, because it is so late." Comfort said to Sephan. "let me take you home, it is too late for you to go alone." He said. "Okay, let me finish my business with Sister Mary." She replied. She went over to the counter and Mary handed her some money. "I will pay the balance on next Friday." Mary told her. "I see you enjoyed yourself?" Mary asked. "yes, very well. He seems to be a nice man, he is taking me home." she told Mary. "Okay, take care of yourself." Mary said to her. Comfort thanked her and went back to the table. "I am ready." She said to Sephan without taking her seat. He took his last swallow of stout and took his car keys as he got up and led the way.

They drove to her house still talking and getting to know each other better. When they got to the house, the place was pitched dark. She took out her little flash light that she always carries on her and turn it on. She thanked him, and they said their good byes. "I will visit you tomorrow if that is okay with you." he stated. "okay" she replied. He waited until she got in the house before driving off.

It was a good night. She kept smiling to herself as she thought the night through. It was too dark outside, and she was also too tired to take a bath. She changed into her night gown and got in bed. She laid on her back looking up at the ceiling, thinking what next, she likes him. She was going over all that had happened until she fell asleep.

It took Sephan 35 minutes to get home. He lives along the beautiful coastline, called Cape Palmas. There was light everywhere. Inside, he took his clothes off and headed for the bath. He whistled all through his bath, he was happy within. He wore his pajamas and jumped in bed. He thought about his next move. She seems to like me too, he thought to himself. He was going to visit her the next day, he was excited. Cool it, his inner voice told him, then he laughed. He felt so happy to fall asleep. His head was getting fill with all kinds of silly things that could go wrong. He kept on turning and moving around until finally sleep over took him.

Saturday was a slow down work day. Although he worked twice as hard as the week days, he was always not in a rush on Saturdays. He got out of bed, brushed his teeth and took a shower. He got to his office and settled in. He went over paper work of the road project, focusing on where they could improve and if the job done was according to schedule and if it was satisfactory. He would then go and inspect the work again and go back to his office and write up the next course of action for the coming week. Inspection took a lot of his time during these projects. It was getting late into the afternoon and he still had a lot to do. He would have to see her today no matter what. She told him yesterday, that she didn't have anyplace to go today, therefore she was going to be home all day. She didn't have a telephone, so he could not have called her. But, he must see her after a long day.

Comfort was laying in bed, the light from the lantern making a faint shadow on the wall. She stared at the ceiling wondering why he did not turn up. Although she did not have anything to offer him when it came to food and drinks but, yet she was hoping that she see him. Did he change his mind after he saw where she lives? She pondered. Well, that was her background. She will not be ashamed of being poor because she did not choose that. Her eyes were getting a little heavy, but she was hoping some how that he would turn up. She tried singing but soon she was fast asleep.

Somewhere in the distance, she could hear a car horn faintly sounding. She twists and turned in bed thinking it was a dream. There was a loud bank at her door making her to jump from her sleep. "who is it?" she asked with her hoarse sleepy voice. Her little sister replied in her dialect "someone is here to see you." She jumped from bed without asking who it was and went outside. There he was standing by his jeep as she stepped outside. "sorry to wake you up, I had a long ang rough day at the office, but I had to see you as promised" Sephan said. "I didn't think it was that late for you" he continued. "What time is it?" She asked. "8;45" he replied. "no, it is not that late, I just dose off to sleep early that's all," She responded. "if you had come earlier you would have seen better, anyway, come in and meet my mother," She said to him. He walked to the front door, but to enter he had to bow his head. He was too tall for their door. On the round table they had, which serve as dinner table and study table depending on what it was needed for, sat Ahdee, as Martha Wleh was commonly called. "Meet my Mom," Comfort pointed to her Mom. "Hello Mama," Sephan said. Martha stretched her hand out for a handshake and nodded her had. English was a strange languish to her. "how are You" Sephan continued. Comfort repeated it in the kru dialect to Martha and she replied. She was alright. Comfort than told her his name and she repeated it. After he had greeted her brother and sisters, she took a bench outside for them to sit.

"How have you been?" he asked her. "fine, how about you?" she asked. "I have not been able to get you out of my mind, other then that, I am fine," Sephan told her. She blushed. She smiles and said "really? What were you thinking about me?" "I will tell you if we can go out for a bit because the mosquito wants to stay in our company out here, I promise to bring you back by eleven." He said. She laughed and laughed. "you are too funny." She said. "let me change into something better." As she dashes into the house before he could say anything. She put on a nice black pant and a ruffled blouse and a flat sandal. She fixed her hair and put on her eye liners. She came out and told her Mom that she was going out for a bit.

"hope I did not take too long" Comfort said. "that is okay" he said. He opened the jeep door for her. She took the bench in the house. She came out of the house and got in the jeep. Sephan drove off leaving the darkness of her home behind them. He took her to Albert Nicol bar which was one of the upskill bar in the city. They enter this large area with all it different corners and seating area. The lights were so deemed and colorful, you could not make up a person face until you came very close to them. He drew her chair out and she sat down. He sat opposite her on a table for two. The waiter came as soon as they were seated and they put in for their drinks. She started to move to the song playing in the bar. "you like to dance it seems?" he said. "yes" she replied. "well if you want to go on the dance floor do not hesitate to ask." He told her. "okay" she said shyly. The waiter brought their drinks and served them. "so, what did you do since I last saw you?" he smiled at her. "a little bit of sewing and helping out in the garden." She said. "really? Do you like working in the garden?" he asked. "yes, I grew up with it. We do small farming, although I do not like the part where we must protect the rice from the birds. That part is tedious. you must keep watching to see which direction the birds will land so you can scare them away. This is sometime under the hot sun. I just like the part we grow the greens and water them and their leaves are so fresh. I like to look at them." "hmmm, that sounds like something I will want to see one day." He said smiling. "I can't imagine you running behind birds" he laughed. "well I do sometimes." She said also smiling.

By the time the night was done for them, they knew a lot about each other. They danced to their favorite song and the night seem to be going very well. By 11:00pm she said, "we have to be going now." He said, "one last dance?" as he stretched out his hand to her. She took it and they got to the dance floor. He put her hands around his neck and put his hand around her waist and drew her closer to him. Her heart scape a beat as she held her breath. She exhaled slowly, too scare that he would hear her heartbeat. As they sway from side to side according to the rhythm of the music, she lay her head on his shoulder and close her eyes. He smells so good, she thought. He took one hand from her waist and put it under her chin. He lifted her face up and kissed her softly. She did not resist his advance as she kissed back. They did not even notice that the music had changed. He took her hand and said, "it's time to take you home." She shook her head in agreement. When they got to the house, he asked her, "when am I going to see you again?" "you are welcome anytime" she said. He smiles and lean over to kiss her. "Thanks." he said and watched her go inside.

"yes!" he said out loud as she closes her front door. Tonight, he was a happy man. He drove off smiling and thinking about their kiss. It made him tingled. That was his baby. He got home, opened his front door and as he was locking it to retire for the night, the telephone started to ring. Who could that be? He thought. He just wanted to lay down and relived what had transpired between he and Comfort. He picked up the phone and he heard "why did you not come to eat your food today?" Catrina asked.

Catrina had not seen Sephan the entire week. He was too busy or occupied to go over. She had plans for the day. She intended to get her time with him to make up for the few days that she did not see him. She had fixed his favorite dish for lunch and had fixed dinner for him. When he didn't show up for lunch she understood but when she could not find him for dinner, that was a concern. She called his friends and they all did not see him, they said. She wondered what had happen to him. She would keep calling his house until she got him.

"I am sorry that I could not make it. Something came up and I had to attend to it" he said. Hoping that she would not press on the matter because he did not want to disrespect her. "I cooked you something you liked, I can bring it over" she said. He asked; "now?", frowning. "yes." she answered. "Please, I will be seeing you tomorrow" he told her. "okay" she said. Something is wrong, she thought. I will find out.

Waking up to a bright sunny day always had a pleasant feeling attached to it. The sun rays piercing the curtains blinded his eyes as he tried to get out of bed. He stretched and smiled. He had a good night sleep. He picked up the phone to called her, then remembered that she had no phone. He wondered how she slept. What was she doing, was she thinking about him, as he was thinking about her? he wondered. He dialed Nathaniel's number. "you are in deep shit my man," said Nathaniel on the other end of the phone. "Catrina was all worried about your where about" he continued. "That is why I am calling," Sephan told him. "let's meet there at 1:00 for lunch." I don't want to go there alone, he said to Nathaniel. "well I hope you have a damn good explanation for her." Nathaniel told him. "come off it, don't I have rights to my live again? She is a mature woman and she would know that it is in her best interest not to dual on my movements." Sephan replied. "Whatever you say boss." joked Nathaniel laughing.

When the got to Catrina it was 10 minutes pass 1:00pm. She greeted them, but you could see from her expression that she wasn't too pleased. He gives her a hug and told her sorry for the day before. "I was tied up with a few things, but I will make it up to you." Sephan told her. She smiles and said jokingly "You will pay for my food you spoil yesterday." "okay, I will even pay for it double." They all laughed. They went straight for the dinner table. Catrina had prepared Collard greens, gravy, with rice and some fry plantain. They jumped right in. The food was delicious. They got through eating and they went to the living room for more chit chat. After some time, he told Catrina that they were going to see a friend and he would be back. He gives her some money as he usually did over the weekend and thanked her. "You promise to make it up to me, but you are leaving." She said. "I will be back soon" Sephan assured her. As they drove off, he told Nathaniel "I am going to drop you off because I am going to see Comfort. Do you remember the girl we saw at Mary's bar the other day that I wanted to talk to and you spoiled my chance then?" Sephan asked Nathaniel. "wow! don't tell me that is what you have been up to?" Nathaniel asked. "well, I bumped into her the other day and we met and we kind of hit it off" Sephan said. "I really like her." He continued. "Anyway, lets meet tomorrow after work at my place and I will tell you about it." Sephan told him. "I will be there" Nathaniel answered. He dropped Nathaniel off and headed to Comfort.

On this beautiful Saturday, Comfort got up in the morning with a smile on her face. She was in a happy place.

She went to the bathroom to freshen up and her entire mind was filled with his image. She wondered if he was coming to see her, so She got ready just in case he was. She didn't want him to come over and she was not looking her best. As the day pass by slowly, she started to feel a little disappointed that he wasn't coming to see her. She saw a car coming from a distance and her heart miss a beat. They didn't get any visitors that had cars. She ran in her room to take one last look at her appearance. She was pretending to not know what was happening outside, waiting to hear her name. One of her sister knocked on the door and she jumped right out. "Hello" She said to Sephan shyly. He opened his arms and said, "no hug for me?" she went into his arms and he kissed her. "where is mama?" he asked. "she and the children are in the back of the house" she told him. She took him at the back to speak to them. She brought a bench for them to sit under the Almond tree that was in front of the house for shade. He held her hand in his, while talking to her and she kept on laughing and leaning her head on his shoulders. They talked into the night. He was telling her jokes from the field which had her laughing a lot.

When he was ready to leave, he got up, went inside and told Martha good night. Holding hands, Comfort walked him to the car. He drew her into him and kissed her slowly at first, she started kissing him and it started to heat up. She pulled back a little for a breath of air. She didn't want him to go, but it was too early in the relationship to tell him so. He did not want to go but did not want to seem too eagled. They stood there, holding each other, kissing each other, and didn't want to let go. Finally, she pulled away as she felt him bulge hard against her body. She said goodnight as he watched her leave him. He got in his car and give a loud sigh. He started the car and as he drove off, He thought about her body against his. He just wanted to hold her there for a bit longer. His mind went to Catrina, he dreaded the fact that he had promised Catrina that he would go back to her house. He just wanted to be left alone and keep the memory of Comfort body pressed against his. He promised, so he drove to Catrina's house. She was at the dining room table when he got in her house. She got up and directed him to her bedroom. She called the house maid to bring them some water, stout and Sephan food in the room. She was locking him in for the evening. He expected that was going to happen. He knew he could not get himself out of this one.

The following days was busy, Monday morning, he got to the office and met a communication concerning the arrival of some equipment from the port of Monrovia. He had to leave immediately to received them. That evening he and James, along with some other employees were set to go on the journey. All this time his mind wondered what was going on with Comfort. At noon he drove to her house to let her know that he was going out for a few days. This time around James drove him. He was disappointed when he got there and was told that she had gone out to her friend's house. He went to his car and wrote her a note. He gave a purse to her mother and gave her siblings some candy money. They were happy and wave good bye as he left.

James drove him to the house to gather some clothes and went back to the office. It would have been nice to see her and kiss her, he thought to himself.

The night was fast approaching as they tore through the road. There were some sleeping already. Sephan laid back in his seat and was kind of quiet, watching the road. It was getting to dangerous time in the journey. The road was so lonely and dark. He had to be strong for all of them. Sleep has no mercy is and old tale. He must watch the driver now, because he would have to take over from the driver if the driver started to fall asleep on the wheel. This was a long journey for them. He loves the road and he loves designing, that was why he study in that field. He felt some joy being on the road. His mind drifted back to Comfort as they continue the drive.

It was getting late and Comfort decided to get back home. When she got home, one of her sister give her the letter from Sephan. "he came here at what time?" she asked. "why did you not run to call me?" she did not wait for the first answer. "he was in a hurry" the girl replied. Comfort went in her room, sat on the bed and opened the note. "My Dear Sweetheart, I have an urgent trip to Monrovia this evening, wish I could take you with me but it is work. I will miss you very much and hope when I get back, we will be able the spend the weekend together." He wrote. She kissed the note as if it was Sephan. With a smile she hugged the letter and murmured, "I can't wait." She laid on her back and put the note on her chest and closed her eyes, thinking about him.

They got to Monrovia after three long days because of the road condition. It took them a week to get the equipment out of the port. Paper work was done from the office to the port back to the office which was an exhausting task. They finally got the equipment's out and got ready to head back. The following week they took off. They line up the equipment's and were on their way Tuesday.

They took less time on their return because they were master now of the roads. Although, the rains made the road conditions even worse than what it was. They knew which areas to go on and which areas to avoid. They got to Maryland on Thursday evening. It was getting late and they were tired. Sephan made sure the equipment's were all parked and locked. Apart from what they had on the road, he was too tired to even eat. He headed straight home, enter the shower and went to bed.

Today the work load was heavy. A lot had to be done at the office and on the field, but he had a good night rest and was ready for work. It was Friday morning and he would pass to Comfort before going to work. He had to let her know that he was intown and would be picking her up after work for the weekend as he had promised. He got ready for work and set off. It was a busy day as assignments were given and reports had to be made during a lot of meetings. Sephan day went so fast that he did not notice the time. He looked up from his desk as James knock and came in. "Daddy, as he usually calls him, should I carry the bag?" James asks. Sephan looked up and said "Oh! what time is it?" not really waiting for James to answer, he looked at his watch. "yes, yes, take the bag, I didn't realize it was this late." Comfort must think that he is not coming, he thought to himself. He got up and stretched himself. He picked up his keys and was out the door.

They arrived at Comfort house at about 8:00 pm. She was pack and waiting. He went inside and greeted Martha. She smiled as usual. Comfort said goodbye to her mother and they left. The ride home was all cozy. He was telling her jokes and she couldn't stop laughing. He would hold her close to him and squeeze her hard. She would shout and start laughing again. When they got to the house, she couldn't believe it. "your house is very nice" Comfort said. With a silly grin on her face. He took her hand and led her to give her a tour of the house.

They finished the tour by taking her to the master bedroom which was the last stop. She couldn't believe that there are people who live in luxury like this. He showed her the bathroom to freshen up. Her things were already brought into the room. She took her bags open it and got what she needed for the bathroom. She closed the door behind her, turned and looked at herself in the mirror. She smiled back at her image. Here she was in this magnificent house with a guy she loves. She got in the bath and figure everything out.

"Are you okay?" Sephan asked. "I am fine, I will soon be out." She replied. "I am waiting for you to come out so that I can go in." He said to her. When the door open, he said "you are so beautiful." "thank you." comfort replied. He leans and kissed her cheeks and went to take a shower.

Comfort lied on the bed and stated looking at the TV. The bed felt so comfortable, soft and silky to the touch. She was feeling good tonight. Something felt special. "is the wine for me?" she asked. He had a glass with a bottle of wine on the bed head table which he had opened and poured a glass for her. "yes love." he answered. She took a sip of the wine and closed her eyes. She didn't drink but knew about wines. This one was sweet, she likes it. This weekend, she was going to live the life. She smiles to herself and threw her head back to continue watching the movie.

Sephan came from the bathroom wearing a white robe around him. "are you okay" he asked. Comfort shook her head in agreement. By this time the wine was turning her eyes a little. He got a bottle of stout out of the small icebox he kept in his room and got in bed. He started sipping his stout as they talked and watched a movie. By the end of the movie, he had had four bottles of stout already.

He got out of bed and turned the lights off. He reached and took the glass from her hand and put it back on the table. He turns to her and snuggle her to him. He looks in her eyes told her that she was beautiful as he kissed her. She kissed him back and snuggle more into him. He caressed her body with his hands, slowly running them along her back to her waist. He would squeeze her hips passionately. It made her tingled and want him more. She did not want him to stop so she sucked on his neck tenderly, caressing his chest, and slowly moving her hands over his tummy down to his manhood. He moans and pulled the cover clothes over their bodies as he slides on top of her. He took off the robe and tossed it to the floor. He rubbed his hands along her body gently, coming up, he cupped her breast and squeezed it with less firmness. She moans with excitement. He kissed her with all the passion he felt for her. He could feel the tightness in his lions as he caressed her thighs. He rubbed his hands softly in her inner thighs and pull them apart. She gasps for air as she felt him slide inside of her.

When she woke up, the room was so bright that it blinded her as she got up and sat in bed. It must be 12:00 noon she taught to herself. The sun made rays under the door as if It was forcing itself through it. "good morning my darling." "did you sleep well? Sephan asked. "Yes, I did." Comfort replied. He kissed her cheeks. "You dressed for work already?" she asked. "I am on my way out. I will check on you at lunch time. Make yourself at home." He told her. "There is tea and breakfast on the table. I will bring lunch at lunch time because I don't want you hurting your pretty little head over it." He said jokingly. She smiles at him as he walked out the door. She heard the car leaving as she was walking to the dining room to get some tea. She took a cup and pore some hot water, thinking all about last night and she smiled. He was special.

The week-end went by so fast, they could not believe that it was Monday already. He was taking her back home this morning. "I enjoyed the weekend and I hope we can spend time together like that from time to time." He said. "I would love that." She replied. He stopped in her yard and held her hands. "I will miss you." He gives her a long kiss and said goodbye. She waved as he sped off to work. She walked in and went looking for Martha Wleh. "Hello Mama." Her mom was glad to see her. Martha was always worried when her daughter left home, but she always wishes for the best as her daughter had a different mindset.

Chapter 6

Catrina was upset. She was in love with this boy who she now hears is crazy about a younger girl. What can she do to stop this? She was feeling humiliated. She had to go with caution because she knows if she pushes too hard it might end her relationship with him. The months pass by and she was losing her grip on him. She was finding him coming over less and less as the months passed. She was too scared now to ask him about Comfort, although she knew her by name, face and some information about her. She had been asking a lot of questions around.

After the Christmas party which made Catrina green with envy, when Sephan openly showed his jealousy toward Comfort by confronting her as she walked in with one of her girlfriends to the party, Catrina decided as an older and more experienced woman, that she would use her maturity to put them apart. She started gathering more information on Comfort from then on.

Every year, two weeks to Christmas day, the elites have parties on different days. It was one of these parties that a friend of Comfort was invited to. She called Comfort and asked her to accompany her to the party. Comfort and her girlfriend enter the party and heads turned. Small talks broke out in various spots. Comfort had turn out again. She was dressed in a short pants, well fitted, a gold sequence blouse, a gold go-go shoes and she wore an afro hair do. She looked so beautiful and her presence was so strong. Sephan turned and realized that it was Comfort and he got angry. Why was she here without informing him that she was going to a party? He just hated the fact that he was not the one who brought her to the party. He walked over to her and told her that they had to leave. She tried to tell him that she accompanied her friend to the party, but he was kind of serious. She told her friend that she had to leave and go with Sephan. All this while Catrina sat on the table with her friends, her eyes fixed on Sephan. She watched Sephan walked to Comfort and witness the entire argument going back and fort between them. She felt so embarrassed, although they did not go together, but a lot of their friends knew that she was seeing him. This made her angry.

In January 1900 and 69, she learned that Comfort was pregnant. She had asked Sephan about Comfort and he had told her about their relationship. She was shaking with anger when she heard about the pregnancy. She called Sephan and said they needed to talk. She said that it was urgent. He rushed over to her house at lunchtime. "Are you responsible for Comfort Pregnancy?" She asked. "Why are you doing this? I thought we went over Comfort issue?" He replied. "I don't want you taking a load that you are not responsible for." She said. "What do you mean by that?" he asked. "Her friend said she is pregnant for the white boy that she is going out with." She told him. She saw confusion on his face. "She told me about the boy, but they are not seeing each other again." He said. "that is what she told you, but her friends said that she is still with him. She even boasted to them that she is going to have her white baby." Catrina continues. Knowing about his jealousy, she watched him caved under her plans. He told her he had to go back to work as he stormed out of the house. She smiled, it would take about eight months for him to find out the truth and a lot of damage could have been done to the relationship.

Sephan was so furious with blind jealousy that he kept away from Comfort for a week. He finally went over to see her but not in a happy mood. She asked him what was the problem? She had not heard from him for a week. He answered poorly that he was busy. "I want us to talk" he said. She brought the bench and they went under the tree. "why did you lie to me about you and the white boy?" "your friends say you are boasting about having his child." "how can you do this" He went on. "where did you get that from? Who are the friends telling you these things? I told you all about that relationship." She said. "why are you listening to people?" "I am listening to people because you go out on your own all the time without me knowing about it. The last party I went to I saw you there. Did you tell me you were going there?" "oh, so you are saying now that I am not pregnant for you?" she said in an angry voice. "I don't know what to think right now" he answered still angry. "until I see that baby, I am not sure" he continues. Tears roll down her eyes as she looked at him. "leave." she said. "is that what you are saying? Instead of trying to prove to me that you are not seeing the boy, you are telling me to leave?" he asked her. "I don't have to prove anything to you. Just leave. When I have the child, you can confirm if its your child." She told him as she walked away. Still in anger, he got in his car and drove off.

The year became very busy for Sephan as the dry season was when the most work was done. Construction had to move at a fast pace as the raining season was harder to work in. He pops in from time to time to see Comfort, but the relationship had lost it flavor. He was always wondering whether Catrina had lied to him or Comfort was the one telling the lies. He wonder why, would Catrina a big woman tell a lie on a girl that she knows about and had not shown any real jealousy towards. He believes that Catrina was very protective of him and just did not want him to be used.

Comfort was also busy with her studies and her business. She was so hard hearted and strong headed, she did not intend for anyone to take advantage of her because she was poor. She hardly gives him much attention because she was hoping for an apology. He was not giving any, so their relationship was getting distance from weeks to months.

By the time the raining season started. Work started to slow down. Sephan was constantly called to Monrovia. Catrina was happy that he was in and out. She was also happy for the lies she had put together that give her an amazing result. She was now like his confident. She would tell him about how, he was a promising young man and should not let a country girl drag him down. In the month of August, he was called to Monrovia urgently. He went to see Comfort, but she had gone out that day. He left a message that he was rushing to Monrovia. His office had sent for him. When he gets back he would see her.

Sephan got to Monrovia and went directly to his office. His boss then told him to go home and take a rest for the week and come the following Monday. He was happy because he needed the rest. On Monday, he arrived at the office. Went through his normal routine of prayer and checking his schedule for the day if he had any. There was an envelope on his desk that read official. He got his letter opener and tore the envelope. He read the content of the letter. He sat down and read it again. He had been promoted to a prestigious position in the government. He was to take office with immediate effect. There was a knock on his door as his boss open the door. Looking in his hands, his boss said "I see that you have seen your letter? Congratulations." "Thank you, sir," Sephan said. "you are the one I should be calling sir now." The boss laughed. "congratulations son, I knew you were going places."

He said. "Thank you again, you have been a father to me here."

Sephan was to take up his office task with immediate effect, that did not give him time to go back to Maryland. He got busy right away. His friends and colleagues heard about his appointment on the news. Some called to congratulate him.

Catrina was quite happy when she heard the news. Nathaniel had gone to give her the good news about Stephan's appointment. They talked about their friend with admiration. When Nathaniel was leaving, she asks about Angela. "she is doing fine." He said. "extend my greetings to her and tell her that I would like to see her before she goes to work today." Catrina said. "okay my dear, will do and you have a good day." Replied Nathaniel. Catrina waved him goodbye as he drove off. She went inside and thought about her next plan of action.

Angela arrived after lunch hour with her boyfriend Nathaniel to meet up with Catrina before going to work. They shared pleasantries and Nathaniel left them. They went and sat in the living room. "We have not talked for a while, you are too busy to that hospital. How are you and the family?" Catrina asked. "We are all fine." Angela told her. They talked like giggling school girls, then finally Catrina said to Angela: "I want to be the first to know about what child Comfort has, please do that for me." "but what is your interest in knowing which child?" Angela asked. "I just want to be the first to know that's all and furthermore Sephan is not here, I think it will be a good thing for me to buy the child a gift." "Okay, I will let you know. Angela assure her. "well, I have to go, don't want to be late." "Thanks for stopping my dear friend." Catrina said as Angela made her way to the door. Catrina smiled as she thought to herself about how her plans were coming together. No little girl will challenge her and get away with it.

Sephan was so occupied with state duties that he asks his friend Tode Davison to transfer his things back to Monrovia and See Comfort. Tode took some items and some money to her. He told her that Sephan would come to see her as soon as he gets the chance but for now he was traveling a lot with the President of the country. Though their relationship was not what it started out to be, but she was hopeful that once the child was born, their relationship will improve.

Months went by without a word from Sephan. She could not continue with school because that was not tolerated in the school system. She then focused on her business which has become difficult because of the pregnancy. Life was just sometimes surprising. She had so much dream and here she was pregnant and didn't even know what was happening in her life. She was happy one minute and in depression the next.

It was early October now and she was starting to have some pains from time to time. She had to go to the hospital soon.

Chapter 7

Catrina put the phone back on the stand without saying goodbye to Angela. Catrina sat up in bed and felt angry and sad. Comfort had just delivered twin girls. She would be the first to talk to Sephan about it. She got up and pace the room. She went over and over what she had to say. It would work. He was jealous, very busy now and believed in her. She had those three things in her favor. He was out of the country, as soon as he got back she would give him the news. She followed his movements, even if it meant that she called Monrovia every day to know what he was doing. She was so obsessed with him that she would even call his boss if she had to.

Martha Wleh had gone home to see the other children and find something for Comfort to eat. When she got back,

Comfort was still sleeping. She set up her food and try waking her up, but she said she was too tired and closed her eyes again.

By the afternoon, the twins were brought in to their mother. "They are so beautiful. Do you have a white person in the family? Their noses are so pointed like a white person nose." One of the nurse on duty said. "my father is light skin with black curly hair" Comfort replied. "I see why they look like this." She handed the child that she was holding to comfort. The child was seven pounds, with curly black hair, light skin, her eyes smiley, pointed nose and a pink lip. Comfort smiled at her. The other girl was placed beside her. She was four pounds, pale skin, thick kinky hair and her head looked battled. She was wrapped so tightly for heat. Comfort looked down at her and asked Martha if the child will make it. Martha assured her daughter that as long there is life there is hope. The nurses showed Comfort how to breast feed the children and they left the room. Martha took up the child lying on the bed and looked at her. She opened the blanket and examine the baby's body. She noticed that the child head was badly shaped. She knew that she had to pay more attention to this child because her daughter was inexperienced to care for this child. She held her until Comfort got through breast feeding the first child and she then handed the second child to her. Comfort was hesitant to take this child because she was afraid that her bones could break if she held her tightly. Her mom helped her tenderly handle the baby. The children went to bed after feeding. Comfort too went to bed with the baby in her arms. Martha took the babies and put them in their bed and sat down.

Catrina called to welcome Sephan who had just come into the country. "how are you dear and how was the trip" Catrina said to Sephan. "It was a good trip, it was very fruitful." "that is good. I believed that you have heard the story about your babies?" Something in him jumped. "has Comfort deliver" he asked without thinking about it. "She has delivered and just as her friends said. She has two white babies. Their skin, their noses and hair can't hide them." She told him. Sephan was so embarrassed and angry that he went silent. "hello, hello, are you there?" Catrina asked. "yes, I am here. Let me call you tomorrow, I have to go" he hung up without waiting for her respond.

Sephan had been upset since his talk with Catrina the night before. He wanted nothing to do with Comfort. How could she do something like that he thought. Forget about her, he comforted himself. He would not let this get to him. He put himself in his work more. Work was the only real thing he knew.

Meanwhile, somewhere downtown Harper city, a couple of nurses involved in the selling and the adoption of children to missionaries from the hospital, were having their usual meeting. "I was thinking, remember the missionary that we call miss picky? She is leaving on Thursday and she still wants a baby." One of the nurses said. "But there are lots of babies, but she is the one having too much problem. All the babies we have shown her she does not want them. If it is left with me I will not even bother with her." The other nurse said. "She is willing to give even more. It is not a bad thing to want to feel connected to a child or see them as special before adopting them." The first nurse said. "There is a girl that have twins and I noticed its only she and her mother. The mother does not speak English. She looks very afraid and I don't think that they can handle those children. She seems to be attached to the very healthy looking one and I don't think she will want to give that one out for adoption. So, we can ask her to adopt the other one" said the third nurse. "I know who you are talking about. The babies are beautiful, but this missionary won't take the one that is looking ill. We will show her the healthy looking one and if she likes her, I have a strategy." Said the first nurse. "There are also two girls there that wants to give their babies up for adoption." The second nurse said. "We will also show those babies to her." The first nurse said. It was time to go to work at the hospital, so they brought the meeting to a close.

The first nurse stopped by a friend's house to make a call. She contacted the missionary and told her about the baby.

"hello, how are you? It's me from the hospital." She said. "yes" said the missionary. "I have this baby that I brought home because her mother pass away while breast feeding her. She is so beautiful and knowing how you have taste I did not want her to stay at the hospital before another nurse had a hold of her. If you are interested, I will bring her in the morning when I get home from the hospital." Said the nurse. "yes, I am interested." The missionary said. "Okay, see you in the morning." The nurse said.

Sephan phone was ringing as he entered the office that morning. He picked it up and it was Tode Davison on the other side. "how are you young man? Haven't heard from you for a while." Tode said. "It has been a hell of a ride my friend" Sephan told Tode. "I learn Comfort had white twins." Sephan said. "I did not hear from her, but I will go and look for her today. Who told you she had white twins?" Tode said. "Catrina called me two days ago and told me" Sephan said. "I will find out today and call you back." Tode told him. "Yes, do that for me." Sephan said. When they got through talking they hung up.

On Wednesday, 5:30am, The nurse came in and took the baby temperature. She told comfort that the baby had a high temperature therefore she had to give the baby a cold shower. "what have you been doing for the baby temperature to be so high like this?" the nurse asked Comfort. She was so scared that she did not know how to answer. The nurse took the baby outside and went to wash the baby. Thirty minutes later, the nurse came and stood at the door of Comfort room with the baby looking limp in her hands. "I am sorry, but the baby is dead. You should have called a nurse when you felt the baby getting sick." The nurse said. "But the baby was not sick, or she did not look sick" Comfort said as she attempted to get out of the bed. "No! dont come near the dead baby. It is not good to go near a dead body because you still have another baby to take care of. The hospital will bury the baby right now." The nurse told Comfort. These things happen, we will take care of it as she turns and walk away with the Baby. As

Comfort sat in bed sobbing and confused, she wondered what had happened. Is it something that she did wrong? She really did not feel the baby skin getting hot. The baby was looking so healthy, now, I don't even know if the other one will make it. She felt so sad. Today is the day that she was going home. Why did this had to happen?

The first nurse logged out. She packed her food basket neatly and hurry out of the hospital yard. She took the Baby home and took care of the baby until the medication wore off. She then called the missionary to come over instead. When the missionary got there the baby was well dressed like a princess. One look at the baby and the missionary was in love with her. "I will take her" The missionary said. The two finished their transaction and parted ways. She would take care of her colleagues when she goes back on duty.

Tode arrived at the hospital that morning to see Comfort but he was told that he could not see her. He asked "why?" and they told him that the doctor give instructions that she was not to be disturbed. He left the hospital without seeing her but intended to come back the next day.

It was time for Comfort to be discharged. The nurse came and brought her bill and discharged card. She looked at the bill and looked up at the nurse. The nurse told her not to worry about the bill as they will write it off because of the lost of her child earlier. Comfort thanked the nurse and give a sigh of relief. She was wondering how she was going to pay the bill as Sephan had not shown up. Martha came back to the hospital and found that the other child had died. She sat on the floor crying. The nurses came and told them that they had to leave since they were already discharged. They told them that crying could frighten the other patients in the hospital. The nurses hurried them out of the premises.

"I did not know that you delivered, it was Sephan who told me and asked me to come and see you. He just got back in the country." Tode said to her. "I went to the hospital yesterday but was told that the doctor order you to rest. I even went to the hospital today and they told me that you had come home." He continued. She did not say anything. She was angry but not with Tode, so she decided not to put her anger on him. Tode asked to hold the Baby and she pointed to the child. "You have to be careful with her" she said. "Who is here with you" Tode asked her. "My mother. She will soon be here." Comfort told him. Tode unwrapped the blanket and examined the Baby. "She is so pretty" Tode said. Tode handed her the Baby and asked, "did you leave Angela Fey at work?" "no, she was not on duty today." Comfort told him. "I learned that she was not working until tomorrow" Comfort continued.

Martha got home and met Mr. Davison. she greeted him as Comfort explained to her who he was in their dialect. Comfort opened the bowl of food that was prepared for her earlier and offered Tode some food. He told her that he was not hungry. She took out some food and started to eat it. She questions Tode for a while and when she was finished eating, she handed the rest to her mother.

Comfort was grateful that Tode came to see her. The baby started to cry, it was feeding time. She asked him to excuse her so that she could feed the baby.

It has been two weeks since the baby was brought home. Today was the naming ceremony of the Baby. Family and friends started to gather at their home. Local drinks and water was serve to the guest. The uncle who was serving as the MC of the program call everyone to attention as Comfort brought the Baby forward to named her. As Comfort took her seat, a smart and active little girl about eight years old rush to Comfort and took the baby hand. "I will name her, I will name her" she said repeatedly. "Her name is IRERA" the little girl said. Everybody started clapping. Comfort wonder who this little girl was but saw her returning to her mother who had come along with Tode. Comfort liked the name. IRERA SOUL. Little children were angels to her, so she believed that it was a name picked by an angel.

Comfort had not heard from Tode concerning Sephan since he visited the last time. She was curious to know what he had told Sephan and what Sephan had said because she had not heard from him as she had hoped. She wanted the ceremony to be over quickly, so she could have a talk with Tode. Comfort could not come to grasp with what had happened with the relationship.????????????????????

Look out for the sequel: IRERA.

CPSIA information can be obtained
at www.ICGtesting.com
Printed in the USA
BVHW03*1050230818
525424BV00003B/15/P